A Secret in the Storm

A great streak of lightning zipped across the sky and the wind almost hurled them off their feet. Sam grabbed his mother's hand. He had never seen a storm like this one.

As they struggled on down, leaves and twigs and bits of straw swirled in the air. There was the dangerous sound of branches breaking; just before they reached the cottage there was another brilliant flash of lightning and, at the same time, right overhead, a deafening crack of thunder. . .

Ready for *more* Young Hippo Adventure?

Henry to the Rescue and Other Stories
Ruth Silvestre

Young Hippo Magic stories to enjoy:

The Little Pet Dragon
Philippa Gregory

The Marmalade Pony
Linda Newbury

My Friend's A Gris-Quok
Malorie Blackman

Broomstick Services
Ann Jungman

Or dare you try a Young Hippo Spooky?

Scarem's House
Malcolm Yorke

The Screaming Deamon Ghostie
Jean Chapman

Young Hippo Funny stories to make you laugh:

Emily H and the Enormous Tarantula
Kara May

Bod's Mum's Knickers
Peter Bere

Young Hippo Adventures for confident readers:

The Outfit series –
The Secret of Weeping Wood
We Didn't Mean To, Honest!
Kidnap at Denton Farm
Robert Swindells

RUTH SILVESTRE

A Secret in the Storm

Illustrated by Peter Bailey

For Thomas

Scholastic Children's Books,
Scholastic Publications Ltd,
7-9 Pratt Street, London NW1 0AE

Scholastic Inc.,
555 Broadway, New York, NY 10012-3999, USA

Scholastic Canada Ltd,
123 Newkirk Road, Richmond Hill,
Ontario, Canada, L4C 3GS

Ash79, Gosford, New South Wales,
Australia

Ashton Scholastic Ltd,
Private Bag 92801, Penrose, Auckland
New Zealand

First published by Scholastic Children's Books 1995

ISBN 0 590 13237 7

Typeset by Backup... Design and Production
Printed by Cox & Wyman Ltd, Reading, Berks

10 9 8 7 6 5 4 3 2 1

Chapter 1

Sam lay on the floor under his bed. Why did things always disappear when you were in a hurry? He'd been looking forward to this holiday for months and now...It had to be there somewhere, his other trainer. Suddenly he spotted it.

"Do hurry up, Sam," called his mother from the kitchen.

"Coming," shouted Sam, grabbing the shoe and wriggling backwards. There was a lot of dust under his bed and he felt his nose tickle.

He put the shoe on, picked up his bag and ran to the kitchen where his mother was rinsing coffee mugs.

"Sam!" she cried. "Where on earth have you been?"

"Under the bed," said Sam. "Don't worry, it'll brush off."

"I hope so," sighed his mother. "Right, let's go." She picked up the big suitcase and locked the front door behind them.

"I hope we don't get burgled, like next door," said Sam.

"It's no good worrying about it," said his mother." Anyway, burglars are after videos or things that are worth a lot of money; and we haven't got any."

Sam smiled. He knew that. Sam was nearly nine. He had bright blue eyes and curly hair

which was usually dark brown but at that moment was covered in dust and bits of fluff. When they got into the lift his mother tried to clean him up.

"You look more like the end of a broom than a boy," she said.

Down and down they went in the lift. Sam and his mother lived on the eighth floor. Sometimes when the lift was out of order they had to walk down. There were a hundred and twelve stairs, two lots of seven for each floor. Walking up was worse.

As they stepped out onto the pavement Sam looked up. Good, the sky was blue and the sun made him screw up his eyes. Almost at once a bus curved round the corner and stopped. Sam helped his mother on with the case.

"Right, now we're on our way," she said, smiling and leaning back in her seat.

"My holiday starts when I'm on the train," said Sam.

Waterloo Station was full of people. There were so many things to look at.

"Don't dawdle, Sam," said his mother. "If you get lost I'll never find you. Sit here and look after the case while I get our tickets."

Sam was beginning to feel excited. There was very cheerful music playing and so many people going in every direction. Some looked

up at the notice boards and down at their watches. Some bought papers for the journey. Some stood in groups eating sandwiches and drinking out of paper cups. And everywhere there were cases and bags; large cases with little wheels on the bottom and bags like brightly coloured sausages that people carried on their shoulders.

Sam could smell doughnuts cooking. He wished he could have one but they were probably expensive and he knew his mother had made sandwiches to eat on the train. They were going a long way.

He was always excited when they were going to the country. They went every summer and when his Grandpa was alive they went for Christmas as well.

He saw his mother coming back with her bright pink scarf tied round her hair. She was looking worried because she hadn't seen him and Sam waved and jumped up and down.

Once they were on the train, Sam's mother handed him a comic. Sam was surprised. "Well we *are* on holiday," she smiled. "And I always bought you comics when I was working."

Sam's mother used to work in an office but the firm had closed down a year ago. Now she only helped in a shop two mornings a week but she didn't earn much money doing that. They hadn't been to the country, to Apple Tree Cottage, for a whole year. The train fare was too expensive.

Sam loved the cottage. Of course it wasn't quite the same now his Grandpa wasn't there anymore. He had been very sad when his Grandpa had died suddenly. He had always had lots of time to spend with Sam. He had always been at the station to meet them in his funny old car.

"Climb aboard the old Rattle-trap, Sam, my lad," he used to shout, while he put their cases in the boot. "You look peaky. Need a bit of Apple Tree air."

And Grandpa would start the engine and off they would speed down the narrow twisting lanes full of flowers and up the other side until they came to the cottage.

And Sam would climb out and run up the path shouting, "We're here! We're here!"

When he was small his mother was always keeping an eye on him in the flat to see that he didn't climb up at the window, or fall down the stairs or over the balcony. But at Apple Tree Cottage he was free. He could run in and out and all round the big garden and no-one would worry and he could make as much noise as he liked.

In the flat his mother was always saying, "Don't thump about so, Sam. You'll give the lady underneath a headache."

And when the summer came and it got hot and stuffy in town she would look out of the window and say, "I don't think I can stand this place much longer," and Sam knew just how she felt.

He looked out of the train window at all the back gardens whizzing by. A dog rushed out and barked at the train. Sam wished he could have a dog but pets weren't allowed in the flats.

He looked at his watch. Only another two hours and forty minutes. His inside turned over with excitement.

"I'm feeling a bit hungry," he said to his mother.

"After all that breakfast?" she said. "Where do you put it all?"

"Grandpa used to say I've got hollow legs," said Sam.

"So he did," smiled his mother. "Well, I think he must have been right. Here you are then."

"Yummy, yummy, ham and cheese," said Sam and took a great bite, opened his comic and felt very pleased with life.

Chapter 2

After an hour they changed to a small train which kept stopping. But at last, there it was, their station! They clunked the carriage door behind them and Sam took the biggest breath he possibly could. He always did that because the air smelled so different.

Now there was no Grandpa to meet them anymore they had to take a taxi.

"Down for the holidays then?" asked the driver, smiling over his shoulder as they bowled along.

"That's right," said Sam's mother. "How's everything down here then?"

"Same as usual," he answered.

"Good!" said Sam and the driver laughed.

"Oh, except for the new lake they're building," he said.

"Well I never," said Sam's mother. "Where's that then?"

"Down the bottom of Cooper's Meadow," said the driver. "Won't bother you, too far away. But my wife's proper fed up with the noise – bulldozers, digging away all day."

"Will we be able to swim in it?" asked Sam.

"I don't rightly know," said the driver. "Well, here you are. That'll be two pounds fifty."

Sam put his bag on his shoulder and then turned to look at his very favourite place in all the world.

"You know, Mum," he said as she came to join him and the taxi disappeared down the lane, "it's really funny but it seems to get smaller every time we come."

"It's not the cottage getting smaller," smiled his mother, "it's you getting bigger."

"I didn't think of that," said Sam.

He looked at the long straight path up to the white front door, the five little windows and the chimney that seemed to lean just a bit sideways, and he felt very happy.

"Just look at all the weeds! The garden's a wilderness!" cried his mother. But Sam thought it all looked beautiful and wild and exciting.

"Can I unlock the door, Mum, please?" he begged. His mother smiled and handed him the heavy old key. Sam turned it once, twice, pushed and the door swung open.

There was no hallway at Apple Tree Cottage. The front door opened straight into the living room.

"Hooray, hooray, we're home!" shouted Sam, dashing in. He threw down his bag and sat himself down in his Grandfather's chair with the velvet cushions and the little stool to put your feet on. He always pretended it was a king's throne.

While his mother unpacked some jars for the kitchen he bounced up and down and gazed around him. Yes, everything was the same. The tall wide fireplace, the funny old clock on the mantelpiece, his grandma's picture and the smoky mirror on the wall.

He got up and looked at his reflection. He poked out his tongue and laughed – but stopped almost at once because he suddenly saw his mother's face behind him in the mirror and he knew that something was wrong. He turned. "What is it, Mum?" he said. "What's happened?"

"I'm not sure, Sam," she answered. "Come and look." Sam's eyes opened very wide.

He followed her into the kitchen. What on earth could it be? The kitchen looked just the same to him. The sink, the dresser with Grandpa's plates and cups, the table, the stove... Sam stopped.

There was a baked bean tin on the stove with a spoon in it. It didn't look as though it had been there since last year, and anyway, they always cleared everything up before they left.

"And see what I found in the bin," she said. Sam looked at the three empty coke tins and the screwed up biscuit wrapper.

"Someone's been in our cottage!" cried Sam. "What a cheek!"

"I think they must have helped themselves out of the cupboard," said his mother.

Sam looked at her. "Who do you think it is? Burglars?"

"They don't seem to have taken anything else," she said. "And burglars don't usually stop to eat baked beans. But I think we'd better go upstairs, Sam, and have a good look round."

Sam stared. "You don't think they're still here, do you?"

His mother shook her head. But at the bottom of the stairs she shouted. "If there's anyone up there you'd better come down now because we're coming up with the dog."

"What dog?" whispered Sam, but she put her finger to her lips. They stood together and listened very hard. There was no sound from above, just a bird singing outside in the garden.

Up the stairs they crept. They pushed open each bedroom door with a rush. Sam didn't quite know what he expected to see. Burglars in bed? He couldn't imagine it. They opened the wardrobes and looked under the beds.

There was no-one there.

"I'm glad about that," she said. "I didn't want to have to do my mother bear act."

"Mother bear?" asked Sam, puzzled.

"WHO'S BEEN SLEEPING IN MY BED?" she growled, and they both laughed and felt better.

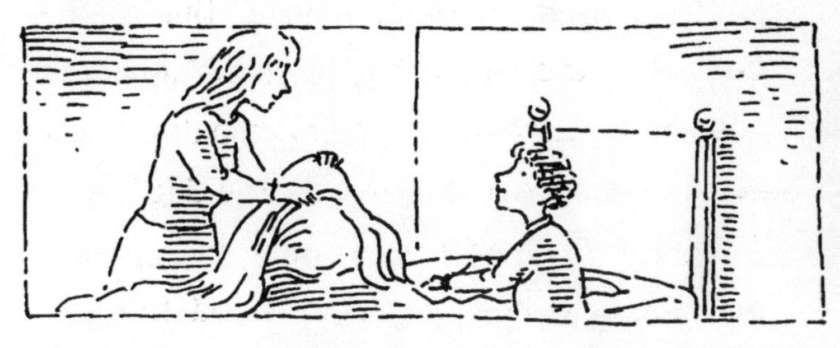

"Help me take the covers off, Sam," said his mother. She looked up at the bedroom ceiling. "Just as well we put these plastic sheets on," she said. "That leak's got worse during the winter. See that damp patch?"

"Never mind the ceiling," said Sam as they folded up the slippery plastics. "Who do you think was in our kitchen?"

"I don't know, love," said his mother. "Let's do the rest of our unpacking. I'll cook us bacon and some sausages later and make a tomato salad, but we'll have to do without the beans."

"That's OK," said Sam. But he knew she was still just a bit worried and so was he.

As he put his clothes in his drawer and arranged his books on his bedside table he kept wondering who it was that had broken in. Perhaps it was someone desperate and dangerous? Perhaps it was someone on the run, even an escaped prisoner? How long had he been coming there and – much more important – was he coming back?

Chapter 3

When Sam and his mother went to bed that night they put a chair against the back door. On the chair they put a saucepan and on top of that, a biscuit tin. On top of the biscuit tin they put a jam jar full of spoons and on top of that, they balanced a tin plate.

"Now, if anyone tries to push the door," said Sam's mother, "that should make enough noise to scare them off."

"And we'll both wake up," said Sam, "and look out of the window and see who it is."

"I expect it was only some kids messing about," said his mother, "but I'll go and get a new lock in the morning and Mr Simmonds will put it on for us. We shan't have any more trouble."

Mr Simmonds lived in the next cottage, which was halfway down the hill, and he did odd jobs, when he was in the mood. When Sam's mother told him what had happened he came puffing up the path that afternoon. Sam sat on the kitchen table and watched him take off the old lock.

"Lord knows how long this old thing has been on here," he said. "And as for this bolt – your Mum should have had me fix it afore you went away last summer. You 'ad a good winter then, young Sam?"

"Not bad," said Sam.

"We didn't see you both at Christmas," said Mr Simmonds.

"No," said Sam. "Mum lost her job and we couldn't afford to come."

"Oh dear, oh dear," said Mr Simmonds, looking over the top of his glasses. "I'm sorry to hear that. There's such a lot of folks nowadays that's got no work.

"There!" he said when he'd finished and the new lock shone brightly on the old back door. "And I've put you on a couple of new bolts. Top and bottom. Now even Houdini couldn't get in."

"Who's Houdini?" asked Sam.

"Famous escapologist," answered Mr Simmonds.

"Famous what?"

"Escapologist," said Mr Simmonds. "Bet you can't spell that."

"You win," said Sam. "Well... I could try: E, S... Anyway what is an esca–, esca-what?"

"ES - CA- POL- O - GIST," said Mr Simmonds slowly. "Chap what makes a living escaping from anywhere. Houdini, he could pick any lock in the world."

"Wow!" said Sam.

"Famous he was," went on Mr Simmonds. "D'you know, they used to handcuff him, put him in a locked box, tie him in a sack and throw him in a tank of water."

"Crikey," said Sam. "Didn't he drown?"

"Not a chance. Before you could count to fifty he'd have all the locks undone and be swimming to the top."

"Fantastic!" said Sam.

"I've got a book about it somewhere," said Mr Simmonds. "I'll look it out for you if you're interested."

"Yes please," said Sam.

His mother came in from the garden with an armful of flowers.

"That looks great, Mr Simmonds," she said, looking at the back door. "Just what we needed."

"Even Houdini couldn't get in here now," said Sam.

"Well," said Mr Simmonds, "whoever it was that's been eating baked beans in your kitchen it wasn't Houdini. He died a long time ago."

"Who do you think it could have been?" asked Sam's mother.

"Blowed if I know," said Mr Simmonds, putting his screwdriver away carefully into his special cloth bag with different slots for each tool. "Probably kids. There's a little gang of them down Snubbs Lane. They gets more cheeky every day. Young Charlie Baxter and that lot."

"Charlie?" said Sam, surprised. He remembered Charlie Baxter. He was never very friendly when Sam first arrived for the holidays but he usually hung about for the first week and then they sometimes went fishing together.

"I can't imagine Charlie breaking into our

cottage," said his mother.

"I wouldn't be too sure," said Mr Simmonds, putting on his jacket. "There's a few new boys in the village now and they egg each other on."

Sam's mother went to the gate with Mr Simmonds and Sam thought about Charlie.

Later on he walked down to the village to see if he could find him. He was pretty sure that it wasn't Charlie who had broken in but he might have seen someone hanging about.

The sun was shining, the birds were singing and Sam couldn't help feeling cheerful in spite of the mysterious break in.

Mr Simmonds was clipping his hedge and his wife was sweeping up the bits.

"Hullo Sam," she shouted. "Down for your holidays then?" Sam nodded. He ran on down the hill. He could hear a droning sound in the distance. It must be the bulldozers over at Cooper's Meadow, he thought, digging out the lake. That would be worth taking a look at later.

The village was quiet. Charlie Baxter was sitting on his gate and he looked bigger than Sam remembered him from the year before. There were two other boys with him that Sam had never seen. One was even bigger than

Charlie and had a fat face under a red and white baseball cap. The other was smaller and dark and wore two rows of badges down his jacket.

Sam walked up to them. The bigger stranger just stared and the smaller one kept sniffing. Charlie Baxter swung his legs slowly backwards and forwards and wouldn't look Sam in the eye.

"Hullo Charlie," said Sam. "How are things then?"

Charlie turned but said nothing. "D'you know 'im then, Charlie? Who is 'e?" asked the bigger boy.

Charlie blushed. His legs stopped swinging. "Dunno," he mumbled.

"Course you do, Charlie," said Sam. "I'm Sam. I can't have changed that much in a year!"

Charlie still said nothing. He looked up and down the road as though Sam was invisible.

"Where've you bin, then?" asked the bigger boy.

"I live in London," said Sam. "I can only come down for the holidays."

"'E stays up at Apple Tree, Fletch." Charlie spoke for the first time. He grinned.

"Oh does 'e? Up at Apple Tree!" sniggered the big boy. "Well, well." He dug the smaller boy in the ribs with his elbow. "We 'as a bit of a go up there sometimes, don't we Garry?"

Garry nodded. His eyes fixed on Sam.

Suddenly Sam felt angry.

"If your idea of a bit of a go is breaking into other people's kitchens, I don't think much of it," he shouted standing straight in front of them. There was a silence. All three boys looked at him. Charlie went bright red but Fletch leaned forward.

"Now look 'ere, Townie," he said. The other two laughed. "You'd better be careful. Comin' down 'ere and accusin' people –"

Charlie slid off the gate. "Come on Fletch," he said. "Let's go."

"But do you know who it was that broke in?" shouted Sam

"Oh yeah, we know," Fletch said. "But we ain't tellin' you, Townie. But 'e'll be back. Then you'll get a fright."

And they raced off down the road laughing and punching each other.

Chapter 4

Sam lay in bed that night thinking about Charlie Baxter and the other two boys. What were they called? Fletch? Yes. And Garry was the other one who kept sniffing. What had they meant? They knew something, but what?

Sam hadn't told his mother about it because he didn't want to worry her. Had it been them who had broken in? Charlie had certainly looked guilty but Fletch had said they knew who it was. How did they know? And why did they say that he was in for a fright? It took Sam a long time to get to sleep and he was very glad that the back door had a brand new lock and two bolts.

The next morning his mother was not in a good mood. Mr Simmonds had to come up again because there was a leak in the lavatory. Every time the chain was pulled water dripped onto the floor.

Mr Simmonds huffed and puffed down on his knees between the lavatory and the bath-tub.

"I used to tell your old dad, you can't go on patchin' things up for ever." he said. "Pipes wears out same as people! It all needs replacing."

Sam's mother sighed and said she was sure he was right but she didn't know how they were going to find the money for all of the repairs that were needed

"But Grandpa always said that he'd make sure we could look after the cottage," said Sam. "He told me lots of times, 'when you need the old nest egg Sam, why then we'll go and find it together'. He said it, Mum. You know he did! What did he mean?"

His mother smiled sadly and shook her head. "Your Grandpa said lots of funny things," she said. "If there ever was a nest egg I should think he spent it long ago."

Sam walked to the gate with Mr Simmonds.

"What is a nest egg exactly?" he asked.

"Just a way of talkin' about your savings."

"Do you think my Grandpa really had one?"

Mr Simmonds scratched his head. "Well, your Grandpa was certainly careful with his money. But him dyin' so sudden like – if he didn't write down where it was – well, I don't see as how you'11 ever know."

Sam sighed. "Everything seems to be going wrong this holiday so far," he said. "First it's burglars and now it's leaky pipes."

"Sam, Sam," called his mother. "Will you go down to the butcher's for me?"

On Wednesday mornings the butcher's van drove into the village and stopped at the end of the street. Sam's mother gave him some money and a shopping list, and he decided to get his old bike out of the shed so that afterwards he could ride over to Cooper's Meadow to see the lake. He knew his bike would seem even smaller this year. Maybe he could put the saddle up another few centimetres.

He crossed the garden through the tall weeds, opened the shed door and went inside.

His Grandpa had kept so many things in it. His "glory hole" he had called it, and whenever Sam had wanted something in a hurry – a piece of wood or rope or a box or a hammer or anything at all, his Grandpa would say, “Let’s have a look in the old glory hole, Sam”, and they would have a great time poking about.

The shed had a window on one side but the glass was very dirty and the light dim. He waited a moment for his eyes to get used to the gloom.

It seemed just as usual, no sign of burglars in here, but it would be hard to tell with all the clutter. There was the pile of logs for the winter, the lawn mower, the buckets and garden tools, his Grandpa’s work bench against the wall. Could that be where he’d hidden his nest egg?

Sam peered into some of the drawers where the nails and screws were kept but they were all rusty. He lifted the tools out of their box but there was nothing. Suddenly he thought that perhaps *that* was what the burglar had been looking for in the kitchen! If someone

knew there was a nest egg they'd certainly be back again. He froze. Was that a footstep outside? His heart raced. He lifted his head, his eyes fixed on the half-open door. But there was nothing. You're just imagining things, Sam, he said to himself. No burglar is likely to come back in broad daylight!

His heart stopped thudding and he took the cover off his bicycle, slammed the shed door, and pedalled to the front gate and away down the lane as fast as he could.

By the time he was halfway down the hill Sam felt better. He decided that the only way to stop himself worrying was to think about something else. So as he was going to the butcher's he concentrated on steak and chips, his favourite meal. By the time he'd got to the village he had made himself so hungry that he had to go to the baker's for a bun.

There was a queue at the butcher's van and when he had bought all the things on his mother's list his saddle bag was heavy, but he did want to go and look at the new lake. He set off for Cooper's Meadow and the bike wobbled as his knees kept hitting the handle bars. There was no doubt about it; his bike was too small.

Sam got off and looked under the saddle. Could it go up? Yes, there was just a few more centimetres to spare. He thought he should have looked for a spanner, and then he remembered why he had left the shed in such a rush and felt a bit stupid. Suddenly Sam looked at his watch. Crikey! It was gone twelve o'clock. His mother would be waiting. He turned round, and as he pedalled back up the lane the shopping seemed heavier and

heavier and the bike smaller and smaller, and when he came to the village his heart sank into his socks. Charlie, Fletch and Garry were standing outside the sweet shop.

"Blimey!" said Fletch. "That the latest bike they 'ave up in London, is it?"

"Where d'you get it then? Out the British Museum?" Garry spoke for the first time. His voice was thin and sounded as though he had a peg on his nose.

Sam said nothing. He tried to keep on pedalling but he knew he'd have to get off soon to walk up the hill to Apple Tree Cottage.

"More like 'e nicked it – out of a nursery school!" Charlie sneered.

"I gotta mountain bike, ain't I Fletch?" Garry said.

"Yeah, an' I gotta BMX," boasted Charlie. "Everyone's gotta better bike than that old heap."

"That's about ready for the dump, that is," said Fletch. Sam jumped off as the bike began to fall. He turned to face the boys.

"Look at little Townie. He's in a rage," teased Fletch, but he backed away.

"You're pathetic!" said Sam. He looked Fletch in the eye. There was a moment's silence.

"You haven't got a spanner have you?" Sam asked suddenly.

"Do what?" Fletch looked stunned.

"A spanner," Sam repeated. "You do know what a spanner is, I suppose?"

"'Course I do," Fletch lowered his head. "What d'you want one for?"

"To put up my saddle," said Sam. "Look. I know it's an old bike. But we can't afford another one. My Mum's lost her job. We could only just afford the fare to get here."

“What about your dad?”

“My Dad doesn’t live with us,” said Sam. “He’s in Canada.”

Fletch dropped his eyes and shuffled his feet. “Well...we might ’ave a spanner,” he said at last.

Garry giggled. “Then, of course,” he said, looking up at the sky, “we might not.”

“Oh, never mind,” said Sam, getting fed up with them all. “I’ll go in and ask Mr Simmonds on my way home.”

“Please yourself, Townie,” said Fletch.

Sam pushed his bike wearily up the hill and he could feel their eyes on his back all the way.

Chapter 5

That night Sam was woken up by the sound of rain lashing against the window. He got out of bed and leaned his elbows on the windowsill and watched the curtain of silver drops running off the gutter. If only he had found a box of gold bars in the shed or a sack full of diamonds he could have the best bike in the world and his mother would stop worrying about money all the time.

He sighed. He didn't think he'd be able to get to sleep again but to his surprise he dropped off almost at once. His clock said ten past eight and the sun was streaming in his window when he woke.

His mother came into his bedroom in her dressing gown. She was carrying a bucket.

"Just look at that," she said. "Half-full in one night. This cottage is nothing but leaks. If it's not the plumbing it's the roof. I don't know what we're going to do."

Sam ate his breakfast quietly. He helped her with the washing up.

"I'm off down to Mrs Simmonds, Sam," she said. "She's going shopping into Dorcaster. I'm cadging a lift. You don't want to come do you?"

"No thanks," said Sam. He had another idea.

"Right," said his mother, drawing on her mouth with lipstick and pressing her lips together, "we won't be long. About an hour and a half."

The cottage was very quiet when she had gone. If only it were true about the nest egg. If only he could find it.

He spent the next hour searching. At first he was excited. What if he found it before his mother came back. He looked absolutely everywhere he could think of but it was difficult when he really had no idea what he was looking for.

He searched on every shelf, in every cupboard and drawer. He took the books out

of the book case and shook each one but all he found were old postcards he had sent from London.

He knew that his mother had cleared out lots of his grandfather's things when he died. She'd probably thrown out the nest egg without realising it, thought Sam sadly as he closed the door of the cupboard under the stairs. It was hopeless. His mother was probably right. It was just one of those things his Grandpa had said and it was all spent years ago.

When his mother came back she made a great pot of soup and some home-made bread. Sam was so hungry that at first he didn't notice that anything was wrong, but then he began to realise that his mother looked very sad.

"What's the matter?" he asked.

She took hold of his hand across the table. "Sam, love," she said. "If there was any other way out I would have found it. Believe me, I've tried."

"Tried what?" Sam didn't know what she was talking about.

"Tried to find a way of keeping the cottage." said his mother. He stared at her in amazement.

"Keeping the cottage? What do you mean? It's ours!" he cried. "Of course we can keep it." He snatched his hand away and stood up, gripping the edge of the table. "What are you talking about, Mum?" he shouted. "I don't know what you're talking about!"

His mother's eyes filled with tears. "Sit down Sam," she said. "Please, love. Let me explain."

Sam didn't want to listen but as she spoke to him quietly he began to understand. She told him about all the things they had to pay to keep the cottage, the insurance and the water rates, the repairs to the roof and the bathroom. "And even the train fare to get down here now," she said. "It's got so

expensive. It wasn't so bad when I had my job, but now..."

"But Grandpa..." cried Sam. "He left us his money! He always told me that he would make sure we could keep Apple Tree for ever and ever..."

His mother shook her head. "Poor Grandpa," she said sadly.

"But he promised!" shouted Sam.

"Oh, Sam. He was an old man. His idea of a lot of money was only a few hundred pounds. It's all gone I'm afraid."

"But what about the nest egg!" shouted Sam. But he knew how hard he had looked and it just wasn't anywhere. His mother stood up and blew her nose.

"You've got to be very brave and sensible and help me. I don't want to sell it any more than you do." She began to do the washing up. Sam just sat at the table. He felt as though he was in a horrible dream. "Now, tomorrow I've got an estate agent coming to look round," went on his mother. "Of course, it may be that it's in such a state no-one will want to buy it."

"Good!" shouted Sam. "I hope he thinks it's the most ghastly cottage in the whole world," and he rushed out of the kitchen, up the stairs and threw himself down on his bed.

Chapter 6

Next morning Sam was still eating his breakfast when the estate agent arrived.

"This is Mr Thornbury, Sam," said his mother, trying to look cheerful.

"Oh, Richard, please," beamed the young man. He had a pink, shiny face and very white teeth and a very white shirt and Sam hated him straight away.

Sam watched his bright blue eyes like laser beams look into every corner of the room as he took a thin gold pen from his pocket and opened a notebook.

"Now let me see," he said importantly, flicking over the pages.

Sam couldn't stand it. "This cottage is falling to bits and it's full of leaks and no-one will want to buy it!" he burst out.

"Oh, Sam," began his mother. She turned to the agent. "My son is very fond of Apple Tree."

"Yes, yes," he said lightly. "Don't worry. I understand completely."

Oh no you don't, thought Sam. No-one does.

"But," said the agent, smiling. "You'd be surprised, young man. This is a very desirable property. Even in its present condition. It's got such character. Can't beat that you know. Takes hundreds of years."

Sam had had enough. He got down from the table and ran outside.

Fletch was walking up the lane kicking a football. That's all I need, thought Sam.

"What's up, Townie?" he said. "You look like the end of the world's coming."

"It is for me," said Sam. He wished Fletch would just go away. But he seemed more friendly on his own. He sat down on the wall.

"What d'you mean?" he asked, bouncing the ball between his knees.

"My Mum's going to sell the cottage."

"Why?"

"We can't afford to keep it. It's full of leaks and things."

"Well – you got another home in London, ain't you?"

"Yes, but," Sam couldn't explain. He felt as though he had a heavy lump on his chest.

"Like it better 'ere than up in London then?" Fletch sounded surprised. "There's nothin' much to do round 'ere." He grinned at Sam. "That's why we ends up eatin' baked beans in empty 'ouses for a bit of a laugh."

Sam looked at him. "So it was you after all," he said.

Fletch grinned again. "Got you worried didn't it? Course it was us. We was up the lane one night and it started to rain so we stood under your back porch larkin' about. Charlie fell against your door and it crashed open. We didn't do no damage."

Sam looked at him. "You didn't have to steal the beans," he said.

"We was hungry," said Fletch. "Anyway what d'you say we forget all about it?"

"OK," said Sam. It didn't seem to make much difference now. But he was glad it hadn't been a real burglar.

"Wanna go down and 'ave a look at the lake?" asked Fletch. "It's nearly finished."

"All right," said Sam. Anything to get away from horrible Richard.

When they turned the last corner to Cooper's Meadow it was so changed Sam could hardly believe his eyes. A year before it had just been a great water meadow with streams running through it where he had gone fishing. Now it was like another world.

"Crikey!" said Sam. "Look at that!" A huge lake sparkled in the sunlight. A row of white boats lay on the far side and men were raking the sand along the new beach. There was a large car park and two long wooden buildings.

"Them's the changin' rooms and offices," said Fletch, "so my Dad told me."

A bright yellow car parked by the gate and a young woman got out. She had short fair hair and wore a red track suit.

"Hi," she said, stopping at the gate. "I'm Hilary. Are you going to join? We'll be open next week. Free day on Saturday, so everyone can have a go. See what it's like. Ever done any sailing?"

Sam and Fletch shook their heads. "Now's the time to learn," she smiled. "What are you called?"

"I'm Sam," said Sam. "And this is Fletch."

She took a roll of papers from her car. "I wonder if you'd do something for me?" she said. "Do you think you could put up these posters round the village so that we get as many people as possible on Saturday?"

"I reckon we could," said Fletch.

"Will we be able to swim then?" asked Sam, looking longingly at the water.

"You most certainly will," she smiled. "See you on Saturday then." And she drove off up the lane. For the next few days Sam was busy putting up posters with Fletch. It took his mind off his troubles, and by Friday, when no-one had come to even look at the cottage, he began to feel a bit more cheerful.

Chapter 7

Saturday was a glorious day. There was a slight breeze and the sun shone from a cloudless sky. There were flags flying over Cooper's Meadow and music playing. A notice stretched across the entrance, COOPER'S MEADOW SAILING & SWIMMING CLUB. There were stalls selling ice-cream and pop-corn and toffee apples. All the instructors wore red caps with COOPER'S on the front and there were crowds of people. The Mayor of Dorcaster arrived wearing his great gold chain. He made a speech about how splendid the whole place was. Sam wished he would hurry up as he was dying to get in the water. At last the Mayor cut a red ribbon and everyone clapped and cheered. A procession of people were shown round the lake to where the sailing dinghies were bobbing on the edge of the water, while those who wanted to swim rushed off to the changing rooms.

Sam loved swimming. He went every week with his school and sometimes his mother and he swam on Sunday mornings. The water was cold and clear.

"It's not like the baths," shouted Sam to his mother, who was putting up her hair in an elastic band. "The bottom feels all soft and sandy. Come on in!"

His mother ran into the water, dived under his legs, shook the water from her eyes and yelled, “race you to the other side!”

Sam suddenly spotted Fletch. He was standing alone up by the office. Sam ran up the beach. “Hey, Fletch,” he shouted, “hurry up and get changed. It’s really great!”

Fletch looked unhappy. "I'm not much good at swimmin'," he said. "Anyway, I ain't brought no trunks."

"Oh, that's a shame." said Sam. "My Mum would soon teach you. She's really good."

Just then Hilary came running up.

"Come on you two," she said. "I've been looking for you."

"What for?" Fletch looked worried.

"You're going to have the first sailing lesson," she said, "because you did such a great job with the posters."

"Fantastic!" cried Sam. Fletch looked even more worried.

"Go and get changed, Sam," said Hilary. "Fletch, come with me and get the life jackets."

Sam and Fletch put on their life jackets and ran down to the boats where Hilary was already standing in the water. The boat looked very small and rocked about a lot.

"Blimey, Sam," muttered Fletch. "I ain't too sure about this, are you?"

"We've got to give it a go, Fletch," said Sam. "She chose us. All the others will be really jealous."

"S'pose so," said Fletch. He looked around at all the young people waiting for their turn. He grinned.

"Well," he said, "at least we can't drown with these things on us."

"In you go," shouted Hilary, "I'll hold the boat."

Sam gasped as the boat tipped up and down. He and Fletch clung together, then steadied themselves and sat down. It was very noisy with everything flapping about in the breeze.

"Keep your heads down!" called Hilary. "And do exactly what I say. You'll soon get used to it."

"I hope so," said Fletch.

Sam laughed. He felt wild with excitement and fear. Hilary waded further into the water, gave a great push and then jumped into the boat. For a moment it seemed as though it would tip right over but as soon as she sat down opposite them it steadied. She leaned over the back of the dinghy. "This is called the rudder," she said, pushing it down. "That's what steers the boat. Fletch, you see that board there, in the middle? That's the centre board. Your job is to push it down gently, when I tell you, OK?" Fletch nodded. He looked very serious.

"Good man," said Hilary. "Right now when Fletch puts down the centre board Sam, you're going to pull this rope. It's called the jib sheet and it pulls up the sail in the front. I'll pull up the main sail and then you'll feel the wind take us. OK? Are you ready? GO!"

Now they were too busy to be frightened. There was a frantic moment of lurching and noisily flapping sails but then the boat tilted up into the wind and they began to move through the water.

"Now we're sailing!" shouted Hilary.

Sam felt as though his heart would fly right out of his chest. It was like magic. It was so frightening and yet so wonderful. He looked across at Fletch. His face was one great grin.

"Well done!" shouted Hilary. "Now Fletch, put your feet under those toe-straps and as you feel your side of the boat rise you can lean out to help us balance."

Next Hilary showed them how to turn the boat. "It's called 'going about'," she said. "We're going to move the front of the boat through the wind. You must remember to keep your heads down."

They did exactly as they were told. Now it was Fletch's turn to pull the other jib sheet and Sam's turn to put his feet in the straps and lean out, as soon as Hilary shouted, "Ready? Going about!"

As she pushed the tiller over, changed sides and the boom swung across they soon saw why they had to keep their heads down. Each time they turned it got easier.

"Wait till I tell my Dad all about this then," cried Fletch.

"Right," said Hilary. "Now we're going to let the wind blow us back. Let go of the sheet and feel the difference."

Suddenly everything changed. The wind which had tugged and flapped so before was now coming from behind their backs and filling the sails without a murmur. All was silence and calm as the boat glided smoothly beneath them and they trailed their fingers in the water. It seemed to take no time at all to get back to where they had started.

Sam's mother ran to meet him.

"How was it?" she said.

"Fantastic!" said Sam. "Wasn't it, Fletch?"

"Brilliant!" said Fletch. "Just brilliant! I can't wait to tell my Dad."

Everyone had a wonderful time that afternoon. As they all dawdled back to the village in the evening sunlight Sam said to his mother, "I wish today could just go on for ever."

"So do I, Sam," she sighed. "But we know it can't."

Chapter 8

Three days later Sam was more unhappy than he could ever remember. He was sitting on the garden wall when a large, grey car drew up outside. Out jumped Richard, the estate agent.

"Hullo Sam old chap!" he cried, as though Sam was his very best friend. "Is your mother in?"

"Yes," Sam glowered and slid off the wall.

Next out of the car came a man with silvery hair, a woman wearing a white dress and a girl about his own age. She was very, very clean. She had long fair hair and wore a pink dress with ribbons on the sleeves, long pink socks and gold shoes. Sam stared at her. As they all looked round the cottage Sam followed behind them. He could hardly bear listening to the woman, who kept saying, "Oh

Charles, look. Isn't that charming!" and "What do you think, Fiona darling?" Fiona darling just looked bored. At least *she* didn't seem to want to buy the cottage, thought Sam, as he escaped outside. When his mother brought them all out to look round the garden, Fiona came up the path towards him.

"D'you think they'll buy it then?" he asked her miserably.

FOR SALE

"I expect so," she said.

"It needs tons of money spent on it," said Sam."Hundreds and hundreds!"

"We're very rich," she said calmly.

Sam stared at her. He'd never met anyone rich before.

"They're always buying old houses," she said. "They smarten them up. Then they sell them again."

He looked at her. Could he make her understand?

"Apple Tree Cottage is not just any old house," he began. "It belonged to my Grandfather. He left it to me. It's very special!"

She turned and looked at it. "It doesn't look very special to me," she said.

When the big grey car drove away Richard looked even more pleased with himself than usual.

"What did they say?" Sam asked his mother, although he didn't really want to hear the answer.

"Oh, they said they are very interested and they'll let me know definitely by the end of the week."

His mother put her arm round him.

"I know, love," she said. "It's very hard. Oh Sam, let's try and forget it for now. I'll cook us something nice for supper."

"I don't want any supper!" shouted Sam. "It's too hot."

"Well, we can have hard boiled eggs and a salad."

"Leave me alone! I don't want any supper. I'm going out!" he shouted. He just wanted to get away. He ran up the lane, on and on. He could never remember feeling so unhappy in his whole life. He knew why his mother had to sell the cottage. He was nearly nine years old and he understood that they had no money and that bills had to be paid. And that it wasn't just bills, it was the roof and the bathroom and the train fare to get there. It was all hopeless. "Oh, Sam. I know how you feel," she had said. But he didn't believe that she really knew that his heart was breaking into bits.

And it wasn't just the terrible aching sadness. He had a dreadful feeling that selling the cottage was all wrong. They shouldn't be doing it. His grandfather had wanted Sam and his mother to look after it as he had done. He had trusted them.

"Don't you forget, Sam my lad," he had said. "Apple Tree Cottage is yours. And the old nest egg – that'll make quite sure you'll be able to keep it." How many times had he said it?

Poor Grandpa, thought Sam, he was just too old to realise what a lot of money it cost these days to fix roofs and things. And of course, he didn't know that Mum would lose her job.

Sam's head was a whirl of desperate thoughts as he climbed the fence and ran on across the top meadow to the big ash tree. It was the biggest tree for miles around. The topmost branches stretched high into the sky but the lower ones reached outwards and down until they almost touched the grass beneath. Sam remembered how he would walk across to it with his grandfather after they had been out picking blackberries, or early in the morning looking for mushrooms. Grandpa would put down his bag and rest his back against the tree while Sam rushed about looking for grasshoppers.

"It's a good old tree," Grandpa would say. "It'll still be here when I'm long dead and gone." Sam had not really listened, but now...

He threw himself on the ground. "Oh, Grandpa, it's not fair!" he said aloud. How could he go back to London and never see Apple Tree again? He felt a great wave of anger and he began to punch the ground beneath him with his fists. His hand hit a stone and it hurt. He began to cry and once he had started he just couldn't stop.

He cried because there wasn't a nest egg after all. He cried because he wished his grandfather was still alive. He cried because his mother didn't seem to understand. He cried because he hated the estate agent and the rich little girl. He cried because he didn't want to go back to the flat and, most of all, he cried because Apple Tree Cottage had to be sold and there was nothing to be done about it.

Chapter 9

Sam didn't know how long he lay there sobbing into the grass. He must have fallen asleep because he woke up to find the meadow in shadow and the sun disappeared over the top of the hill. He shivered and rolled over onto his back. There was a wind blowing now and the great ash tree was whispering as if to warn him.

He scrambled to his feet, brushing off the sticks and leaves. He looked at his watch. Crikey! It was nearly half past eight. His mother would be wondering where he was.

He began to hurry down across the meadow. He could feel the wind getting stronger. He looked back at the ash tree standing out against the darkening sky. It was very strange. The topmost branches were all streaming towards him like flags but the bottom ones were swirling and tossing like giant, angry arms.

The wind began to howl, softly at first then louder. He heard the first rumble of thunder and in the distance, his mother's voice. "Sam! Sam, where are you?" she was calling.

"I'm coming!" he yelled.

He began to run. Almost at once a flare of lightning cracked across the sky.

"One, two, three," Sam counted as his Grandpa had taught him. "Four." Crash! went the thunder. Rumble, rumble, rumble...

Only four miles away, Sam said to himself as he raced along. He knew that storms could travel very fast.

"Sam!" it was his mother again, nearer this time.

"I'm coming, Mum!" he yelled as the next flash of lightning dazzled his eyes.

The first heavy drops fell on his back and his head and in seconds he could hardly see for the rain. It came down like a wall of water. It ran off his hair, down his neck, into his eyes

and mouth. It smelled good and tasted good but it was very, very wet.

At last he reached the edge of the meadow and climbed up and over the high gate. His feet slipped on the wet bars. He lost his balance and fell down the other side into a muddy hole. Scrambling out he ran on. Halfway down the lane he met his mother, the water dripping off her long hair.

"Oh, Sam," she cried. "What a state you're

in! I was so worried."

"I'm OK," shouted Sam. The wind was getting wilder and wilder and the thunder louder.

"Come on, run! Let's get home!" yelled his mother.

A great streak of lightning zipped across the sky and the wind almost hurled them off their feet. Sam grabbed his mother's hand. He had never seen a storm like this one.

As they struggled on down, leaves and twigs and bits of straw swirled in the air. There was the dangerous sound of branches breaking; just before they reached the cottage there was another brilliant flash of lightning and, at the same time, right overhead, a deafening crack of thunder.

And with it there was another sound. A crash of something falling. Sam and his mother looked up at the cottage just in time to see the top half of the old leaning chimney disappear through the roof.

"Oh, Sam!" his mother was crying. "What are we going to do now?"

"Let's get inside, Mum," shouted Sam. "Come on."

They raced up the slippery path and in through the front door. Then they stopped. Sam and his mother, soaked and filthy and frightened, just stood and stared.

Bricks and cement from the chimney had crashed through the roof and then through the ceiling and lay scattered over the hearth rug. The clock from the mantelpiece lay broken on the floor. Sam's grandmother's picture hung at a crazy angle, the glass smashed to pieces. And it was beginning to rain in the living room!

As they stood there, frozen for a moment in horror, it got worse until a curtain of water was falling all along the mantelpiece and into the fireplace.

"Help me move everything!" his mother shouted. Together they dragged all the furniture back and carried some of it into the kitchen.

"We'd better go upstairs," said his mother. "Here, take a torch. I don't want you switching on any lights. It might be dangerous."

Halfway up the stairs they had to clamber over another pile of rubbish from the roof.

Although the thunder seemed to be further away now, the rain was pouring into his mother's bedroom. They pushed her bed into the driest corner.

"We'll get out the plastics," she said, "and cover everything up. What's your room like?"

Sam went in and shone the torch around.

"Dry as the desert," he called.

"Thank goodness for that," said his mother, dragging in her mattress and her duvet. "I'll have to sleep in here with you."

She emptied out all the buckets and then they went downstairs and made hot chocolate.

"One good thing," said Sam, sitting perched on the table. "I don't suppose those horrid rich people will want our cottage now, don't suppose anyone will want it. Except me, of course."

"Oh, Sam, don't start!" said his mother. "I'm worn out. Let's just go to bed, OK?"

Chapter 10

When Sam opened his eyes next morning, for a moment he wondered where he was. Then he realised that he had pushed his bed across the room, and then he remembered why. His mother was fast asleep on the floor beside him. She looked very tired.

He slid quietly off the end of his bed and tiptoed down the stairs. Halfway down he had

to edge his way around the lumps of plaster which had fallen in the storm. He looked in horror at the huge hole in the staircase wall. One of the stairs was completely smashed in. He stepped over it carefully.

The living room looked even worse in the daylight. Sam sat on the damp floor, his arms round his knees. Whatever would happen to it now? Oh Grandpa, he thought, it's a good job you can't see it this morning. And what would his mother say when she woke up? Perhaps he'd better make her a cup of tea.

He put the kettle on and moved about quietly in the muddled kitchen. He usually only did breakfast in bed on her birthday but he knew she would really need cheering up today. While the kettle boiled he got out the mugs, the milk and sugar. He made the tea and two slices of toast and jam.

He tried not to rattle the tray as he started up the stairs but it was very awkward when he got to the pile of broken plaster. He turned the tray and tried to slide past sideways. But as he took the next step he forgot about the broken stair and with a crack his foot went right through it.

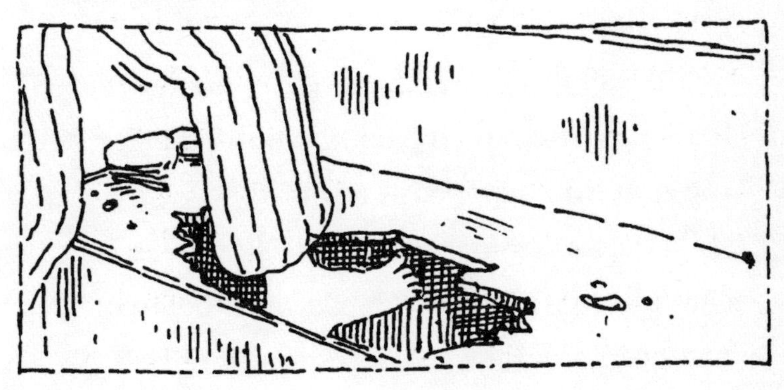

"Help!" he shouted as the tray lurched. He managed to steady the sliding breakfast but his foot seemed to be stuck.

"Sam?" It was his mother. "Are you all right?"

"It's OK," he shouted. "Well – it's not really. I can't move."

His mother came down the stairs in her dressing gown. "Oh, Sam, love. Breakfast!" she said, taking the tray. "What a nice surprise. But what have you done?"

"My foot's stuck. I can't..."

"Don't try to pull it out," said his mother, putting the tray down on the top stair. "You'll get splinters."

She bent down and, covering his leg with her hand, she pulled back the broken piece of the stair and snapped it right off.

"Thanks," said Sam. As he lifted his foot carefully out, a dusty piece of paper which had been stuck to the bottom of it fell off.

"What's this?" he said, picking it up. His eyes grew wide. "Mum! Mum! Look!" he cried.

In small neat letters was written

For Sam from his Grandfather.

"Wow! Mum! Do you think it's the nest egg?" he breathed.

"I've no idea," said his mother. They both leaned over and looked into the hole. It went down a long way and was full of dust, jagged bits of wood and cement, and broken plaster.

"Whatever it is, it's underneath all that stuff," said Sam.

"Careful," said his mother. She grabbed the back of his pyjamas while he leaned into the space beneath the broken stair.

"I've got something!" he shouted, but it was only half a brick. Next came two lumps of cement.

"I suppose this is part of the poor old chimney," said his mother taking the pieces from him. "Can you see anything else?"

"There seems to be a sort of shelf underneath," said Sam. "I can reach it but one end is blocked off with something heavy. I can't move it."

"Come out a minute," said his mother. "I'll get the torch."

Together they peered into the hole. Sam was right. There was a shelf with one end blocked off by the fallen chimney but behind it, just visible in the torch beam...

"Crikey! Mum! It's a box! It's a box!" shouted Sam. His mother moved the torch closer.

"And look! There's a small box on top of the larger one," she said.

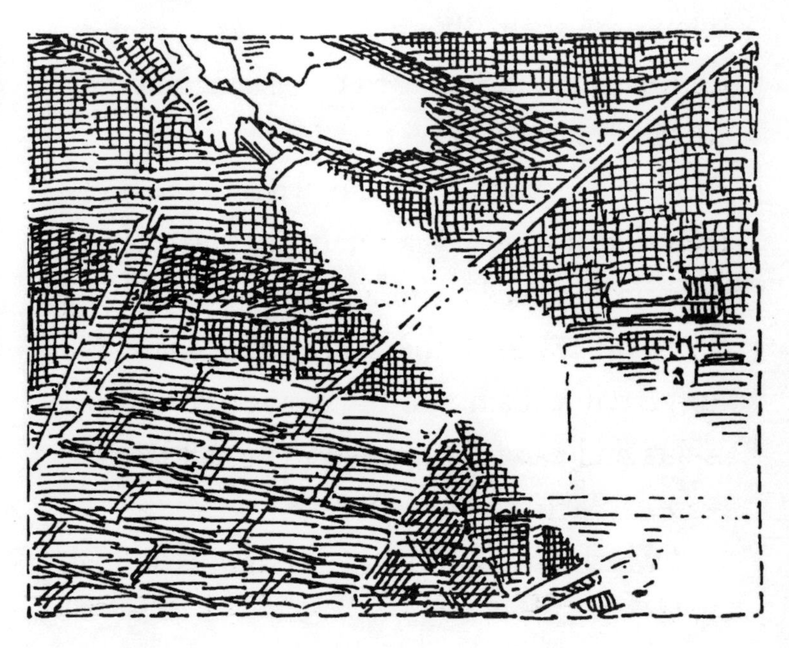

"We might just be able to lift that one through that little space there," said Sam.

"Hold the torch. I'll try. My arm is longer than yours," she said. She moved her fingers along the shelf. "It's no good. I can reach it but my hand is too big to pull it out. You try."

Sam braced his feet against the wall and pushed his shoulder right down into the hole. His fingers closed around the little box. Gently he pulled it through the narrow space.

The tea and the toast were cold and forgotten as Sam and his mother sat on the stairs and carefully opened the small leather case.

"Wow! Mum!" breathed Sam, "Is it real gold?"

"Yes," said his mother quietly. "That watch belonged to my Grandfather. I haven't seen it for years and years. I thought Dad had sold it long ago. And these rings were my mother's."

"Are they worth a lot of money?" asked Sam.

"I suppose they must be," she said. "But I should hate to have to sell them." She slid one of the rings onto her finger and looked at it dreamily.

"Mum," shouted Sam, "We've got to get the other box out!"

They both tried pushing the broken chimney but it wouldn't budge.

"Let's look in the cupboard under the stairs," she said. "We might be able to see from there."

"Right, come on!" yelled Sam and he scrambled over the pile of rubbish and ran down the rest of the stairs. But when they had taken out the wellington boots, the broom and the vacuum cleaner and the step ladder and the ironing board, there was nothing but muddy stains on the cupboard ceiling. It seemed quite solid.

"We shall just have to get dressed and ask Mr Simmonds to have a look," said his mother. "Oh – today's the day he goes to his gardening club."

"I can't wait," said Sam."There must be a way in. How did Grandpa put it there?"

Sam got a stool and looked very carefully all round the top of the cupboard. His heart was beating very fast. The cupboard ceiling was made of boards which had once been painted white. Between each board was a dusty groove. Sam ran his finger down each one. Suddenly he stopped. Beneath the dust there was something else, something which shone.

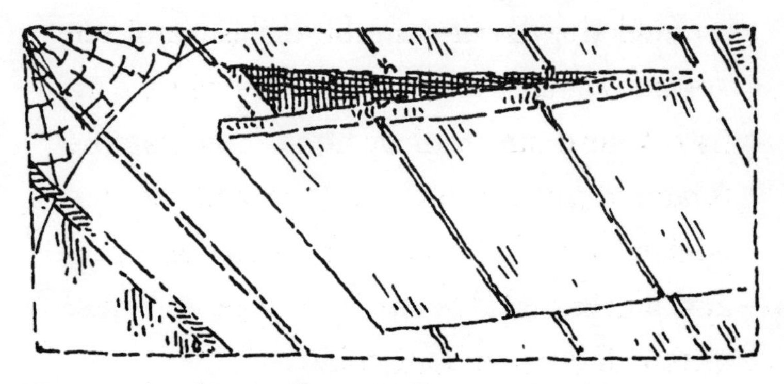

It was a hinge, a brass hinge. His heart beat even faster. He ran his fingers down the next groove and the next and the next, and suddenly his fingers touched a nail and a trap door dropped open. "Mum! Mum!" he shouted "I've found it! Bring the torch."

Together they lifted out the box, which was quite heavy.

"What d'you think is in it?"

"Goodness knows. Let's take it to the kitchen." But when they put the box down they found it was locked.

"There's loads of old keys in the drawer here," said Sam, "Quick, Mum!"

They tipped out the table drawer and, sure enough, amidst all the muddle were five old keys. But none of them fitted. Sam couldn't bear the suspense. There was also a small screwdriver and he slid it under the rim of the box and forced it open.

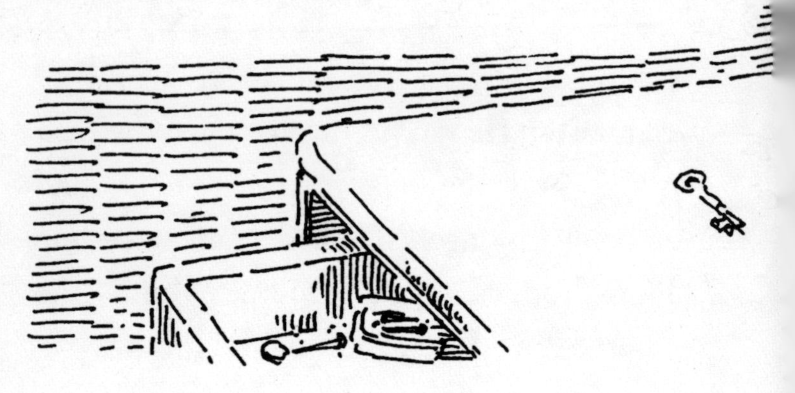

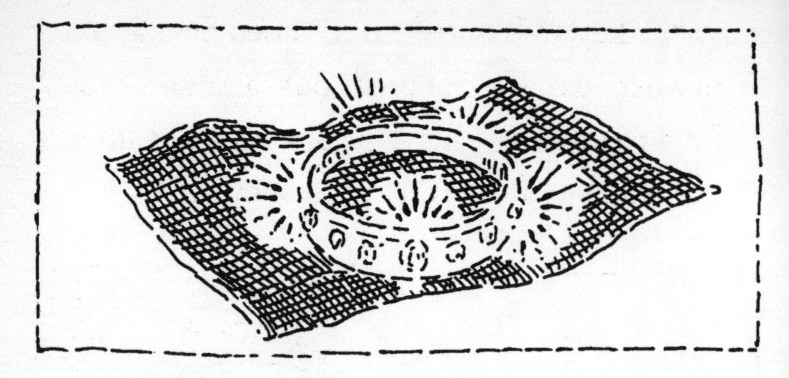

Inside was a leather bag with a folded piece of velvet lying on the top. Sam's mother gently unwrapped the velvet and held up a beautiful bracelet. Sam saw the colours flash.

"Are those real diamonds?" he asked. His voice squeaked with excitement.

"Yes, I think so," his mother whispered. "This belonged to my Grandmother. I can just remember her showing it to me when I was very little. A rich lady left it to her when she died. I'd forgotten all about it," she shook her head. "I can hardly believe all this." She picked up the leather bag and untied the string around it.

"Crikey! What are those?" cried Sam as his mother, gasping, poured out a shower of bright coins into her lap. She scooped up a handful and dropped them one by one.

"Sam," she said at last in a strange voice. "I think these are sovereigns. There must be over a hundred here. Oh Sam!" She suddenly burst into tears. "Poor Grandpa, he did have a nest egg after all – in his secret hiding place – and he died so suddenly he didn't have time to tell us about it. If it hadn't been for the storm we would never have found it."

Sam watched the tears running down her face and felt his own eyes prickling. He flung his arms around her. "Grandpa was right all the time, wasn't he? We'll never have to sell Apple Tree now, will we Mum?" he cried.

"No Sam," she said, wiping her eyes, "I think we're saved. Saved by the storm." She blew her nose. "At least, we'll have to see what all this lot is worth, but gold sovereigns today are very valuable." She hugged him hard. "Come on, let's get dressed and go and find out."

Chapter 11

The jeweller in Dorcaster telephoned to London and as soon as Sam's mother heard how much Grandpa's boxes were probably worth she called into the estate agent. Sam thought that after finding the secret, it was his next favourite moment, when they told Richard their good news.

He just stared at them, his mouth turned

right down at the corners.

"Well, if you change your mind..." he sighed at last.

"I don't think we will," said Sam's mother, smiling.

"Not a chance!" said Sam.

That afternoon everyone came to help them mop up and clear away all the damage from the storm. Fletch brought Charlie and Garry and they all loaded the rubbish onto the wheelbarrow and pushed it down the garden.

Mrs Simmonds came up to help Sam's mother carry the bed out into the sunshine and Mr Simmonds stretched a big blue plastic sheet over the hole in the roof.

Mr Simmonds' son, who was called William and lived in the next village, came with his mate Tom and they set about repairing the chimney and fixing the slates.

The days flew by and soon there was only one week of the holiday left. Sam began to feel sad at the thought of leaving.

One afternoon Sam's mother came back from the village looking thoughtful.

"Sam?" she said, after supper. "How would you feel about staying here?"

Sam gasped. "You mean... live here? Not go back to London?"

"Yes, I saw Hilary today and she offered me a job. Of course we'd have to go back to clear the flat and fetch our things but..." She paused and looked at him very keenly. "Would you mind? The job's only part time, down at Cooper's Meadow – but it might be full time later on. What do you say?"

For a moment Sam said nothing. His mind just raced round, then, "Brilliant!" he shouted. "Brilliant!"

"Are you sure?" said his mother. "You'd have to change schools. You'd have a longer journey on the bus..."

"I wouldn't mind that," said Sam.

"And it's a bit quiet down here in the winter you know."

"We'd bring our television."

"Of course, but you've got all your friends in London, and..."

"I've got friends here too, now," said Sam. "And the others could come down and stay sometimes, couldn't they?"

"Of course," smiled his mother.

"And can I have a dog?"

His mother laughed, "I'd quite like a dog myself. I want you to be happy."

Sam thought he had never been so happy. All at once everything was quite perfect. He ran out into the garden. It was just getting dark. The first star was out. He looked up at it. He thought about his Grandpa and how much he loved him. "Thanks Grandpa," he whispered. Suddenly he heard someone bouncing a football up the lane. He ran to the gate. “Fletch! Hey Fletch,” he shouted. “Wait till you hear the news!”